Dear Parents:

Congratulations! Your child is taking the first steps on an exciting journey. The destination? Independent reading!

STEP INTO READING® will help your child get there. The program offers five steps to reading success. Each step includes fun stories and colorful art or photographs. In addition to original fiction and books with favorite characters, there are Step into Reading Non-Fiction Readers, Phonics Readers and Boxed Sets, Sticker Readers, and Comic Readers—a complete literacy program with something to interest every child.

Learning to Read, Step by Step!

Ready to Read Preschool–Kindergarten
• big type and easy words • rhyme and rhythm • picture clues
For children who know the alphabet and are eager to begin reading.

Reading with Help Preschool–Grade 1
• basic vocabulary • short sentences • simple stories
For children who recognize familiar words and sound out new words with help.

Reading on Your Own Grades 1–3
• engaging characters • easy-to-follow plots • popular topics
For children who are ready to read on their own.

Reading Paragraphs Grades 2–3
• challenging vocabulary • short paragraphs • exciting stories
For newly independent readers who read simple sentences with confidence.

Ready for Chapters Grades 2–4
• chapters • longer paragraphs • full-color art
For children who want to take the plunge into chapter books but still like colorful pictures.

STEP INTO READING® is designed to give every child a successful reading experience. The grade levels are only guides; children will progress through the steps at their own speed, developing confidence in their reading. The F&P Text Level on the back cover serves as another tool to help you choose the right book for your child.

Remember, a lifetime love of reading starts with a single step!

Text copyright © 1998 by Gail Herman.
Cover and interior illustrations copyright © 1998 by Lisa McCue.
All rights reserved. Published in the United States by Random House Children's Books,
a division of Penguin Random House LLC, New York.

Step into Reading, Random House and the colophon are registered trademarks of
Penguin Random House LLC.

Visit us on the Web!
StepIntoReading.com
randomhousekids.com

Educators and librarians, for a variety of teaching tools, visit us at
RHTeachersLibrarians.com

Library of Congress Cataloging-in-Publication Data
Herman, Gail, 1959– .
The lion and the mouse / by Gail Herman ; illustrated by Lisa McCue.
    p.   cm. — (Step into reading. A step 1 book.)
Summary: In this retelling of an Aesop fable, an adventuresome mouse proves that even small
creatures are capable of great deeds when he rescues the King of the Jungle.
ISBN 978-0-679-88674-7 (trade) — ISBN 978-0-679-98674-4 (lib. bdg.)
[1. Fables. 2. Folklore.] I. McCue, Lisa, ill. II. Aesop. III. Title.
IV. Series: Step into reading. Step 1 book.
PZ8.2.H43 Li 2004   398.24'529757—dc21   2002014817

Printed in the United States of America   38 37 36 35 34 33 32

This book has been officially leveled by using the F&P Text Level Gradient™ Leveling System.

The Lion and the Mouse

by Gail Herman
illustrated by Lisa McCue

Random House 🏠 New York

PART 1

Little Mouse.

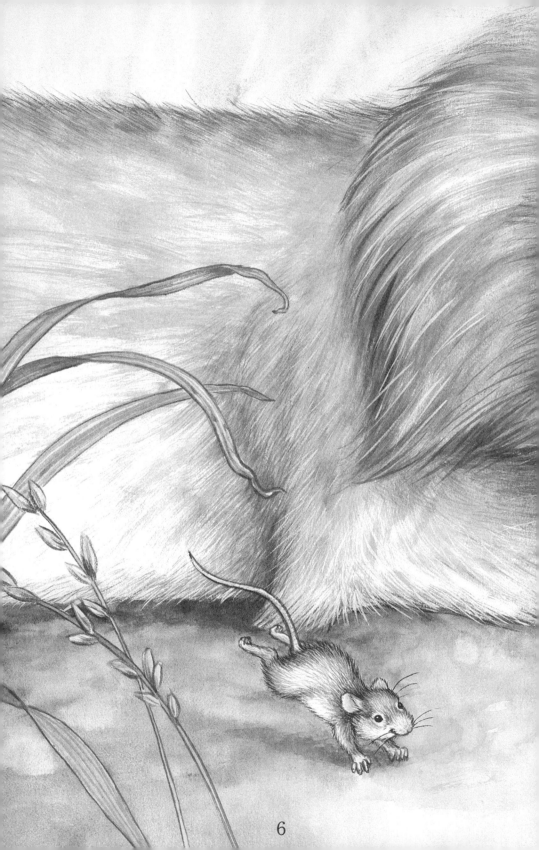

Big Lion.

Big, big trouble!

"Let me go!"
begs Mouse.
"Someday
I will help you!"

"YOU help ME?"

says Lion.

"Ha, ha, ha!"

But Lion opens his paw.

He sets Mouse free.

PART 2

Big Lion.

Big net.

Big, big trouble!

ROAR!

Mouse sits up.

He follows that roar.

"Help me!"
begs Lion.

Mouse starts to chew.

He chews

and chews.

He sets Lion free!

Lion does not laugh
at Mouse now.
Now he knows...

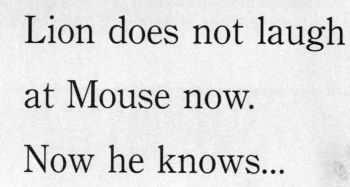

...even the
littlest Mouse
can help
the biggest Lion.